Acknowledgments
Designed by Liz Antill. Photographs by Tim Clark and art direction by Roy Smith. Models made by Whoopee! Productions Limited and backgrounds illustrated by Martin Aitchison.

British Library Cataloguing in Publication Data

Hately, David
    The tale of Jemima Puddle-duck.
    I. Title   II. Potter, Beatrix, *1866-1943*
    823'.914[J]
    ISBN 0-7214-1095-2

First edition

Published by Ladybird Books Ltd Loughborough Leicestershire UK
Ladybird Books Inc Auburn Maine 04210 USA

Text and illustrations copyright © Frederick Warne & Co., MCMLXXXIX
Based on *The Tale of Jemima Puddle-duck* by Beatrix Potter
copyright © Frederick Warne & Co., MCMVIII
© In presentation LADYBIRD BOOKS LTD MCMLXXXIX

Printed in England

The tale of Jemima Puddle-duck

Based on the original and authorised story
by **Beatrix Potter**

adapted by David Hately

Ladybird Books
in association with Frederick Warne

60p.

Jemima Puddle-duck was annoyed. The farmer's wife had taken away her eggs and put them under a hen to hatch.

"I don't need any help from a hen!" quacked Jemima to her sister-in-law, Mrs Rebeccah Puddle-duck. "I want to hatch my own eggs."

"Whatever for?" Rebeccah quacked back. "You would never be able to sit still on a nest for twenty-eight days, Jemima. You would let the eggs get cold. You always were a bad sitter."

But Jemima Puddle-duck had made up her mind. One fine spring day she put on her shawl and a poke bonnet. She ran downhill, her shawl flapping, and then jumped off into the air.

She flew beautifully when she had got a good start, and she soon reached the woods. There she waddled about in search of a nice dry nesting place.

She rather liked the look of a tree stump amongst some tall foxgloves.
But seated on it was an elegant gentleman reading a newspaper.

The elegant gentleman had black-tipped ears, sandy-coloured whiskers, and a long bushy tail. Jemima wondered who he was. "Quack?" she said, tipping her head to one side.

The elegant gentleman lowered his newspaper and saw Jemima Puddle-duck. "Have you lost your way?" he asked politely.

Jemima explained why she was not able to lay her eggs at the farm, and complained about the hen. "I'm looking for somewhere dry to nest," she said.

"Come with me!" cried the bushy-tailed gentleman. "I know just the place!"

He led Jemima to a little house. It was very ramshackle and had two broken buckets, one on top of the other, instead of a chimney.

At the back of the house was a
tumbledown shed made from old
soap boxes. The polite gentleman
opened the shed door and showed
Jemima in.

The shed was full of feathers! Jemima was quite surprised to see so many.

But she made herself a comfortable nest, while the gentleman with sandy-coloured whiskers waited outside.

When it was time for Jemima to go home, the elegant gentleman promised to take good care of the nest.

"I love eggs and ducklings," he said. "I shall be proud to see a fine nestful in my shed."

Jemima Puddle-duck visited her nest every afternoon. She laid nine large greeny white eggs. Then she announced that she would begin sitting on them the very next day, and that she would bring enough food to last her until the eggs were hatched.

The elegant gentleman was delighted. "Before you start," he said, "let's give ourselves a dinner party as a treat."

"When you come tomorrow," he continued, "bring some herbs to make a stuff…er, a savoury omelette. We need sage and thyme, parsley, mint and two onions. I myself will bring the lard for the stuff…er, the omelette."

Jemima Puddle-duck was such a simpleton. Not even the mention of sage and onions made her suspicious.

Next morning she went round the garden, nibbling off bits of all the herbs used for stuffing roast duck. Then she went to the farm kitchen and took two onions from a basket.

But Kep, the clever collie dog, saw her. "Where are you off to with those onions?" he asked, and Jemima told him the whole story.

Kep was very interested in the gentleman with sandy-coloured whiskers. He asked lots of questions about the wood, and wanted to know exactly where the shed was.

Then he went off to the village to find some young friends of his. They were two foxhound puppies who lived with the butcher.

That afternoon Jemima set out, for the last time, with her bunches of herbs and two onions in a bag. When she reached the ramshackle house, the bushy long-tailed gentleman seemed rather nervous.

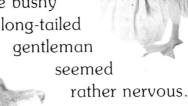

"Give me the herbs and onions," he snapped. "Go and look at your eggs while I prepare the ...er, the omelette. Then come straight into the house. And be quick about it!"

Jemima had never heard the elegant gentleman speak so sharply. She went into the shed feeling surprised and uncomfortable.

While she was in the shed, Jemima heard the pattering of feet outside. Someone with a black nose came sniffing at the foot of the door and then locked it! Jemima was very frightened.

A moment later came the most awful noises – barking, baying, howling and squealing.

In a little while, Kep
opened the shed door and
let Jemima Puddle-duck out. He had a
bite on his ear, and the two foxhound
puppies were limping.

B ut there was no sign of the foxy-
whiskered gentleman.

Unfortunately, the foxhound puppies rushed into the shed and ate the nine large greeny white eggs before Kep could stop them. Poor Jemima had to be taken home. She was in tears because of those eggs.

In June she laid some more eggs, and this time the farmer's wife let her keep them. But only four of them hatched.

Jemima said that this was because of her nerves.

But, as Rebeccah Puddle-duck knew very well, Jemima had always been a bad sitter!